Hundred Lives Of A Poet

Rahul Gangwani

AF518100

BlueRose ONE.com
Stories Matter
NewDelhi • London

BLUEROSE PUBLISHERS
India | U.K.

BlueRose ONE.com
Stories Matter
NewDelhi • London

For permissions requests or inquiries regarding this publication, please contact:

BLUEROSE PUBLISHERS
www.BlueRoseONE.com
info@bluerosepublishers.com
+91 8882 898 898
+4407342408967

ISBN: 978-93-7018-964-5

Cover design: Yash Singhal
Typesetting: Namrata Saini

First Edition: May 2025

About The Book

This debut collection promises to be more than just verses on a page. It is an invitation to witness the world through the eyes of a seasoned observer, a compassionate healer and a keen interpreter. Readers can anticipate poems that weave together intellectual insight with heartfelt emotion, offering glimpses into the interconnectedness of all things. Expect to find reflections on universal truths that have long captivated poet's attention.

With a life dedicated to learning, teaching, healing and understanding the intricate patterns of the universe, poet Rahul Gangwani's foray into poetry is a natural extension of his remarkable journey. This first book is not just a collection of poems; it is a testament to a life lived with intention, wisdom and a deep appreciation for the beauty and complexity of existence. It is a voice that promises to enlighten, comfort and inspire.

"A poet lives hundred lives,
temporarily if not forever,
Every emotion is an eternal story,
Celebrating and shining in it's own glory."

-RAHUL GANGWANI

Acknowledgements

Publishing *'my first book'* is an experience which I'll experience 'only once' in this lifetime. This is a transformation of my school time hobby into a professional journey. I started to compose poems in 2001 when I was only 13 and it took almost 24 years to become a published poet. At this moment, I would like to dedicate my book to the most important persons in my life- My Mother- Mrs. Lakshmi Gangwani and My Brother- Mr. Sushil Gangwani. It has been their blessings and prayers which have brought me so far.

"Love You Mummy!!"

I also would like to express my gratitude towards my friends and seniors like Mr. Sudam Korde (Bade Sir), Mr. Swapnil Korde, Mrs. Sunita Joshi, Mr. Yogesh Hadpe and Mr. Jitendra Sonje. It has been their love and support which has helped me grow. A special mention for my best friend Satyajeet Thakur and my grandmother- Mrs. Chandra Talreja who have always stood with me through my thick and thin.

Some people who are no longer with me also must be acknowledged at this moment like Late Maulana Farooq Sahab and Late Ramesh Samel Sir. Their divine blessings have always been my strength.

My teachers and mentors too tremendously contributed to shape my personality into who I'm today. I would sincerely acknowledge the contributions of Mrs. Chaitali Biswas, Mrs. Parveen Sheikh, Mrs. Swami, Mrs. Jyoti Naidu, Mrs. Prema Katale and Mrs. Nasreen Patel.

Last but not the least, I would also express my gratitude to my ideals like Late Anand Bakshi Sahab (renowned poet and lyricist) and Sudha Chandran ji (famous actress and dancer). Their talent, dedication and contribution towards art always remains inspirational in my heart.

A Prayer

Genre- Philosophy/Spirituality

Theme- A Holy Prayer

O Mother Earth! I'm having my meal for which I thank thee,
But some brother of mine might sleep hungry, so please see.

Bless my Syrian friend with security from the jaws of untimely death,
Help my Korean brothers escape from atrocity bullet.

Gift peace and love to my Nigerian relatives (your children) with thine holy hands,
For someone awaits food in far Sahara lands.

Help my teenage US cousins conquer the teenage lifestyle pressure,
Bless them not with drugs but meditation and healthy leisure.

My Afghani and Arabian uncles and aunts want to live with their beloved and dear,
I pray that you grant their wish and let joy replace terror and fear.

My supper is over, it's time to sleep,
May all rest daily peacefully, whenever you peep.

For me there is no black, no white, no Indonesian, Canadian or Australian,
I believe in no rich, no poor but see human as human first as I'm an INDIAN!!!

Animals

Genre- Philosophy/Social/Wildlife

Theme- Degradation Of Human Qualities

Have you looked into their eyes?
"Eyes are gateway to the soul!", do you know?
If you do, the only thing you will witness is innocence!
An innocent child resides in all of us,
It is sleeping in humans but in them it's active and awake.

Sit with a dog- your pet and see the difference,
You still think of the world, the money and desires, but he (or she) thinks only of you- the master!
Get the difference or not?
Ever thought or not?

Have you ever heard of an elephant revolting? A horse turning rebel?
Well Never! Atleast not a domestic one.
They however would have if they were humans,
Thank God, they are not!

Eyes of a carnivore are full of anger and fury,
But he needs to be so, cause he has to hunt!
But why does a human hunt another one for power, money or lust ?
Atleast a lion or tiger don't conspire and politicize their existence!

Chameleon changes colors to live,
But humans change more than the poorly blamed creature,
And that too for selfish motives,
Why blame the helpless soul?

Reptiles carry poison, so we hate them,
But humans carry more poison in their veins, how to hate them?
We do know which one will toxify our blood,
But how to identify the toxic blood relation?

You feed litter to a cow or buffalo,
Yet it will feed you with milk.
Does it fail to do it's duty?
But what about a man who expects extra salary,
But doesn't wish to fulfill his basic duties?

A mandarian duck preaches life lasting honesty,
Can a man teach the same so effortlessly?

Humans choose as per their convenience,
While insulting, call others 'donkey' or 'bitch',
But while glorification call 'tiger', 'peacock' or 'the emperor of the jungle'.
Well... still you need animals! Don't you?

So next time you tag someone as an animal,
think if you are targeting or crowning the other one?
Because the animals carry 'Godliness' of naturality which we don't!
We can't!

Glossary- *1. Mandarian ducks live with the same partner forever. As one partner dies, the other one remains single till last breath*

2. Emperor of jungle- lion

I Love Maths

Genre- Humour

Theme- A Student Disliking Subject Maths

I love you Maths,
just as a sheep loves a carnivore.
You always inflict thy wrath as a hunter,
I being a herbivore.

You asking me to always find 'x',
makes me look like an ass if not a zebra.
Did you have serious issues with your 'ex'?
Please tell Mr. Algebra!

With my family and friends, I have a better 'equation',
than the 'simultaneous' or 'quadratic' ones for sure.
Whenever the page flashes a question,
my sheet goes through scribbling pain without a cure.

Why does the angle in Pythogoras Theoram have to be right?,
Coz my answer is always wrong!
Let me continue my 'Triangular Fight',
Motivating myself with a marching song.

How can I forget my nightmare- 'Trigonometry',
where finding the answer is a gigantic issue.
Why did you add fuel to fire when I already have Geometry?
Which tests my body's each cell and tissue.

My mind is always engaged in imaginary problems,
'first man has 2 chocolates and second has one'.
Ok, I study so I have to deal with sums,
But why the hell when it comes to chocolates, I have none?

'Time and Speed' add to my misery,
every now and then they increase my heartbeat,
Expand the list, make way for 'Profit and Loss',
can I just quit my examination seat?

I respect Aryabhatta for his invention,
as it is mostly decorating my answer ie 'Zero'.
But experiencing silver lining of shameless motivation,
I feel like a purely proud villain and not a superhero!

My love for Arithmetics will always go through 'multiplications',
however it's value still will be 'negative'.
Untill I'm accepted by the family of 'additions and subtractions',
my 'divided' marks won't let me be 'positive'.

<u>Poet's Words-</u> *This poem is dedicated to one of my inspirations-* ***Mrs. Sudha Chandran*** *whom I consider a warrior conquering the biggest adversity the life could throw at her. She happens to be a 'Bharatnatyam' legend, a veteran Hindi Film/TV actress and has worked in multiple regional progarmmes as well. But, all these achievements are a result of her unbroken spirit and never quit attitude. Indeed, her historic performance as the evil Ramola Sikand in TV Serial Kaahin Kissi Roz (2001-2004) lives in my memories since teenage. It inspires me till date.*

With love,

To Sudha Ma'am

The Dancer – I (Shattered Dreams)

Genre- Biography/ Inspiration

Theme- A Real Life Story Of A Classical Dancer

Poetic Speciality- 1. Every second line is an Inversion

2. Poem's first couple of lines and last lines are similar yet contradictory

I was a girl, sweet and sixteen,
Flying were my ambitions at the peak of 'age of teen'.

A hardworking dancer, passion ran in the blood of mine,
As temple was my music, my Church, my holy Shrine!

My friends defined me as a beautiful dove or a rejoicing peacock,
Waited eagerly my treasure of achievements to unlock.

Salsa, Samba or Ballad, a lot to cover,
Faith possessed I, being an art lover.

When the music played my world was only the stage,
Surely, world would I conquer for I was a sensation at a young age.

But lightning struck and my dreams were shattered,
Came about sunset, when sunshine truly mattered.

A normal travel from one city to another down south,
Horrifying accident it turned into causing wounds, hand to mouth.

The road accident snatched away my dance – my life,
No boundries knew my pain, as if heart cut with a sharp knife.

My leg was infected with poison, couldn't destiny be softer?,
"The leg either or the girl?", said the doctor.

Parents with 'rock on the heart' chose my life, with limb being cut,
"Almighty Oh! Let no parent face such crossroad with if and but!"

Next day, I woke up and life was a nightmare,
Weeping were my parents endlessly, yet showering affection and care.

Now I was a girl, sweet and sixteen,
Dead were my ambitions at the peak of the 'age of teen'.

The Dancer – II (The Hope)

Sorrow was morning, sadness was night,
Miserable was life, months were gloomy without any light.

Eyes around me were sympathetic, disappointed or even made fun,
Hopeless was I, as I couldn't walk fast or run.

But my parents remained unmoved just like an ocean rock,
Knew only almighty, what life had to unlock?

One day a close relative introduced concept of artificial foot,
Visible was hope in the eyes as in thoughts the idea began to root.

'Fighter parents' and I now met a caring warm doctor,
Funny was he sometimes, was he an actor?

Many sittings, check-ups, specialists took measurements,
Too young to understand was I, as we bought new garments.

With one artificial leg, I started to walk holding a stick,
'Ouch!' from my swollen leg bleeding was I, making me sick.

The journey was tough, the road rough, yet I was a fighter,
Torch was I, ready to be lit, parents being 'the lighter'!

Days passed, so did weeks, fortnights and months too went,
Drastically improved movement of mine, say 70 if not 100 percent.

Slowly, steadily one day I practiced my easy steps of old dance,
"Wait!" Realized I, that I could continue my old romance.

Now hopefulness was morning, satisfaction was night,
Happening was life, with new ray of light.

The Dancer- III (The Rise)

I went to my teacher-my mentor saying, "My illness was the question but my spirit is the answer." Replied he, "Come child! Defeat the odds, reboot, you are born to be 'a dancer'!"

Since that day, I trained fighting irresistible pain,
Believed I strongly, my struggle won't go in vain.

Sometimes I battled bleeding, while sometimes blood clots,
Painfully firm was I, everyday's practice meant a lot.

Days, nights, weeks and months full of agony and rage,
Moist eyes or small smiles felt I, as the calender turned each page.

Three years had passed as I was training,
To lose had I nothing, I was only gaining.

Finally, one day, my Guru came with affirmation to be on the stage,
In front of live crowd, would be I, breaking the shackles and cage.

Mom-dad agreed believing as a dancer I had re-emerged,
Time was it, to bring out the paradise long back submerged.

I practiced for hours and hours far from thirst and hunger,
No chance had I to fumble or create any blunder.

But deep down lied the anxiety awake in the hearts of ours,
"Failed if, then what?", the function would last for hours.

The fears, worries and unsaid tension rose as time looked,
Inevitable was overthinking, as the auditorium was booked.

Tomorrow was the show and none of us could sleep at night,
Line bottom- "Can we win tomorrow's last war not just fight?"

The sun rose, now the time would not halt,
Mixed were emotions, every now and then flowing with salt.

With all thoughts cluttered, we reached the hall,
Broken was glass, I was again in front of all.

Costumes, plannings and last minute touch up already done, it was showtime,
Unforgiven would be mistake, as it wasn't mistake but crime.

With teary eyes they blessed me- my parents and Guru,
Said I, "I will meet you only when I get through."

The curtain raised, audience and I saw each other,
"Gosh Oh! This is my comeback, perhaps there wouldn't be another."

Introductory speech delivered and the music was played,
With knife could tension be cut, or perhaps even blade.

I began and today I can't recall what happened after I first glanced,
Only remember I that for next few hours I only danced, danced and danced.

In the concluding moments, the music closed and so did my act,
Applauds thunderous and standing ovations, the audience did react.

Mom kissed and hugged while overjoyed dad remained near,
Clapped sir his heart out, my mentor, my dear.

Audience continued to clap, I felt like a princess without Cinderella gown,
Choked with emotions now were all of us, could finally breakdown!

The salty water ran down on my cheeks originating in flooded eyes,

"Conquered had I, my failure and darkness met their demise!"

My mentor said, "Your illness was the question but your courage is the answer!"

Continued he, "You have defeated the odds, you are born to be a dancer!"

The Dancer- IV
(The Legend)

I was reborn that day, today I admit being my own announcer,
Down walking the memory lane, I became a dancer.

Years later, my life is full of work with A-listers,
Includes resume of mine, top actors, directors and ministers.

My family-my biggest support- my hubby,
Likes he when I'm thin or even chubby.

Trophies, medals, awards- I have a lot to showcase,
Enjoying am I, my life's brightest phase.

Today I again dance like a peacock, my every dance is celebration,
High flying am I in sky, dove being my inspiration.

I was reborn that day, I admit being my own announcer,
Down walking the memory lane, I became a dancer.

You don't belong here...

Genre- Philosophy

Theme- Life Experiences/Work/Career

If the everyday routine becomes unbearable,
the duties beyond tolerance,
the output unsatisfying,
the future appears blur, uncertain and unclear,
it's time to understand, you don't belong here!

If the growth stunts,
the flame of passion diminishes,
the lethargy rises,
the silence of emotions replaces cheer,
it's time to understand, you don't belong here!

If authorities disgust,
the orders turn into rebel,
the persona of yours is taken for granted,
the feeling of a caged eagle or locked lion intensifies
as you peer,
it's time to understand, you don't belong here!

If inner voice is heard loud enough,
the shell cracking is 'a must',
the universe sends messengers and signals,
the present door needs to be closed to open the future gate my dear,
it's time to understand, you don't belong here!

Poet's Message- *"Quit a job which doesn't let you develop and kills your dreams. You deserve to grow. No salary is big enough which forces you to live in a toxic workplace. Go, leave and do something that nurtures you. Who knows you might be born to work wonders!"*

The Jungle Elections

Genre- Humour/Satire

Theme- Politics/Democracy

The Election Commission of the jungle announced polling dates,
Now, it was time for new pals, alliances and mates.

The non- believers of miracles saw the tiger being polite to the goat,
While the elephant started to woo the sheep and dogs for vote.

The happiest were the 'opportunist' monkeys ,
justifying change of parties as change of clothes,
Like jumping from one branch to another,
Old ideologies demolished followed by new oaths.

The snakes, scorpios and allegators/crocodiles- the underworld's increasing demand was clear,
The 'politicians' made sure that the innocent voters- buffaloes and stags felt the fear.

The poor migratory birds were attacked for being 'outsiders',
Thus 'a hatred injection',
While other party offered them 'security' for votes,
Thus 'a political affection'.

The wolves and foxes were on opposite ends as the strategist characters,
While eagles in one, crows in another performed the role of spokesperson cum actors.

The regionalism, racism, casteism and religious fanaticism flourished in the 'developmental speeches' of the leaders,
No sun, no soil, no rivers or rains, they considered themselves as the 'world feeders'.

The 'Big Shot' enterpreneurs- hippo and rhino were the financers behind the curtain,
The builders- woodpeckers and rats had their role and it was pretty certain.

With the new dawn, the polling date arrived in the jungle lives,
Some males contested themselves, while some hid behind their wives.

The 'Judgement Day' appeared with the celebrations in Mr. tiger's apartment,
But the majority was still away by a few seats as per the announcement.

The cheetah- as always the fastest offered his party seats for government of coalition,
While he grabbed some 'creamy' ministeries, Mr. elephant had to be content being 'Leader of Opposition'.

Minority leader- porcupine had emerged victorious from his seat but, by his partymen was let down,
With marginalized constituencies was assigned the opposition by the jungle town.

The animals noticed 'vote for cash' or alcohol distribution as a corrupt tool,
'Victory is Victory by Hook or Crook' was the golden rule!

The false promises of the Government were exposed very soon,
The entire jungle collapsed as after two months it was failure of monsoon.

The old story repeated itself as the goat had to bear the tiger's hungry stare,
And which caste or religion voters were lagging behind- who would care?

'Let's multiply our private wealth with public funds' was the common rhyme,
As it is, who is bothered about the voters unless it's 'Next Election Time'?

Disclaimer- All characters in this poem are imaginary but their resemblence to any country's democratic system or politics or government is not a co-incidence but intentional!

Innocent Complaint

Genre- Humour

Theme- Children/Fun

Ya Mom! I am complaining…keep the score,
If any of complaints are invalid…kindly ignore.

Why am I the only one who disturbs your household chore? (atleast you feel so…)
Why you say "Just one more spoon,sugar!" and feed me four? (food)

Why other children are sweet? Am I sour?
Why every evening while playing you pull me back through the door?

Why do you have to remind me "Don't spill, don't pour!"?
How many instructions do you have in your store?

When was the last time you scolded dad when a page he tore? (I always get fired!)
Have you ever laughed at granny? I haven't seen that too for sure.

Why should I entertain your friends? They laugh at me which I can't ignore.
Am I a clown? It's the simple question deep in my heart's core.

So many suggestions and advices, these commands I completely deplore,
"Don't run!", "Don't laugh!", "Wash your hands properly!", to name just three or four!

But mom, how long will I hold my frown, I'm not sure,
The moment you kiss or hug me...I'll love you even more.

-Your Beloved Son

Poet's Note- The poem attempts to raise it's voice against the social curse called girl child infanticide.

"Let the Girl Child Live!"

Girl Child

Genre- Social

Theme- Children/Emotions/Realism

In the mother's womb rests the unborn child,
Unknown to the outside seasons- cold, hot or mild.
Growing like a moon, she starts to speak,
"Hi Mom! I'm growing stably week by week."

"Love you Mumma! Though I haven't seen you,
You are very pretty and tough and I know it's true.
And dad must be tall, strong and macho in real life,
You are so lucky mummy being a hero's wife."

"I want to see the light, it's too dark in here,
I want to talk to you openly, right now your voice is not clear.
I wish to see the world with my pair of eyes,
I want to sleep on your lap and breasts where my comfort lies."

"Perhaps time will fly or arguably run,
Moon will change, while constant will be sun.
From the oyster particle, I will be a pearl,
Within months I will be a school girl."

"I will play, do my homework with help of yours,
May be sometimes will disturb you while doing household chores.
I would want to visit circus, movies and for sure zoo,
Whenever I'll get a chocolate, I'll save half for you."

"I'll try to be a good daughter and a good sister, I promise,
I'll try to be second mother to my younger sibling, I promise.
I'll teach my younger brother to walk holding my finger,
Don't worry! He will sleep sound when I'm near the swinger."

"Years will fly or arguably run,
Moon will change, constant will be sun.
I'll be a diamond transforming from the pearl,
By now I would be a college girl."

"I'll sing, dance and study with lots of friends,
But I promise no nightouts and no boyfriends!
I will fulfill your dreams, staying awake day and night,
I will make you proud , bring joy and delight."

"I'll be a lawyer, engineer or even an actor,
Can't rule out being a singer, dancer or director.
But always my parents would be the skylight above,
Assets come and go, my richness will be your love."

"Now ready I would be for life's next stride,
With ring in my finger, I would be a bride.
Feeling gratitude I'll welcome the new phase of my life,
With your blessings, beginning a new role of a wife."

"He (my husband) would be my prince in my heart's kingdom,
He's cute! He's naughty! How mean! Ah! The thoughts are random.
His moustache thorns, while lips petals of a flower,
In bed, kitchen and living room, affection and love I'll shower."

"I'll embrace his relations too, his mother will be my mother,
I'll cook and serve delicacies, his brother being my brother.
I'll provide support when papa will struggle to walk,
I'll explain the stuff when they would be too weak to talk."

"Years would fly or arguably run,
Moon will change, constant will be sun.
Now I'd be a necklace, no diamond or pearl,
I'd be a woman and mother of two, not a girl."

"My younger ones will make me run after them with soup and milk,
But when they fall asleep tired, life will be as smooth and pretty as silk.
On Sundays, we would relax and rejuvenate in nearby meadow,
I would not be original but forever your shadow."

"I'll bring up my babies with values just like you,
But still will take care of you and dad. Yes, I'll do!
I'll be a support to my husband in his highs and lows,
I'll be a cool shade of banyan tree when hot air blows."

"To be a good daughter, sister, wife and mother, I'll always strive,
But all relations, my wishes would be granted ONLY IF I SURVIVE.
It's too dark in here, please let me see the light,
Please don't kill me within, pushing me forever in dark light."

"If you end my journey before it starts, I'll be furious and angry on you,
But I'm your and dad's part, so will forgive and still love you.
I'll come in a new form experiencing new parents in some other place hot, cold or mild,
I'm born to be a daughter- home of relations and emotions because I'm the GIRL CHILD!"

Rest in Peace!!!

Genre- Philosophy

Theme- Social/Human Behaviour/Motivation

Don't be a prisoner of what is no more,
The dead moments why are you preserving?

May be he dumped you, may be she cheated on you,
But those lost, not you!
So have a 'grand funeral' of the 'dead relationships',
And let it REST IN PEACE!

May be a friend double crossed you,
May be a 'bunch of cowards' insulted you,
Become a tiger, so that they are no better than dogs,
Have a 'dominant funeral' of the 'dead friendships',
And let it REST IN PEACE!

May be you failed in some exam,
May be you couldn't get selected in the sports,
Become a 'ruler' of 'your ground',
So that tomorrow you mock that failure in the face,

Have a 'polite funeral' of the 'dead attempts',
And let it REST IN PEACE!

May be you lost your job,
May be you were fired or had to quit,
Become an 'opportunist' and look at ex-bosses with a scary stare,
Have a 'professional funeral' of the 'dead work',
And let it REST IN PEACE!

May be you disrespected your parents,
May be you broke up with your lover,
Regret every bit of it and release the anguish,
Have a 'painful funeral' of the 'dead mistakes',
And let it REST IN PEACE!

May be you consumed alchohol,
May be you were an addict,
Re-establish yourself, rehabilitate yourself,
Have a 'forever funeral' of the 'dead habits',
And let it REST IN PEACE!

May be you suffered 'bad luck',
May be 'destiny was cruel',
Become a warrior, conquer your destiny,
Have a 'royal funeral' of the 'dead defeats',
And let it REST IN PEACE!

The 'dark cell of mind' where you still exist- you need to burn,
Break the cage, be free,
Live in the present, plan for the future,
Only preserve 'Gold of the past',
Destroy everything else,
Have a 'final funeral' of the 'dead past',
And let it REST IN PEACE!

The Indian Farmer

Genre- Social

Theme- Agriculture/Nationalism/Farmer's Life

The sky turns grey, it's the first day of June,
The eyes turn upwards calling silently for monsoon.

Then comes the moment, first drop falls and then they multiply and multiply further more,
The dust rises, the aroma spreads, wet become the plains, plateaus and even the shore.

In the north, the prayers are chanted on the banks of Ganga Maiyya (mother),
While the south sees the eagerness of the cultivator ready with his Naiyya (boats).

Brahmaputra and Mahanadi in the east all set with full force to flow,
While Godavari and Tapi in the west are looking for their "Get…Set…Go!!"

Wherever he is, his (farmer) heart is racing to pick up his weapon,
The dream is the same no matter which region.

The first contact between droplets and the soil indicates hopes fulfillment very soon,
For every 'son of soil' knows that draught is a curse and rain is a boon.

Ignoring father's illness and resources for daughter's marriage will be a crime,
And no excuses can help, for bank loans grant no time!

It's he, his yoke and bullocks who pull the plough to sow the seeds,
Cutting the brown, red, black sheets of soil, walking through stones and weeds.

The bells tied around the neck of 'farmer's best friend' swing carelessly,
All over India, they compose the sweetest celebration melody endlessly.

The blessing of nature comes today when the rivers romance the seducing flood,
Now for him (farmer) there is no stopping whether it's wound, injury or blood.

Ignoring last night's back-ache and fever of his wife,
He is going to work now and then, for this is his life.

The drops of sweat and rain water at times get mixed becoming one,
He yet can't express his gratitude to the almighty, it's his only fun.

The happy man as he looks has however, paid a huge cost,
Tears roll down his cheeks as he recalls the friends he lost.
(the farmers who died in previous years)

One of his relatives hanged himself as he could not survive the hard time's tide,
Another one lost the battle as the flooded river demanded sacrifices far and wide.

But the 'show will go on' from dawn to dusk everyday,
As the unseen-hidden treasure awaits it's time to appear and stay. (food grains)

The south will give pearls (rice) and north will give birth to golden wires (wheat),
The cutting and harvesting of the priceless rewards will commence around Diwali fires.

He knows no boundaries, walks with time and has no armour,
He is the 'feeder of the nation' known as 'the Indian Farmer'.

.... And I Met A Stranger!

Genre- Love/Romance

Theme- Love Story Of A Girl

After visiting the Taj, India Gate and the shrines of Himalayas, the journey was about to end,
With every passing moment my heart desired for the vacation to extend.

Fifteen days of the trip were about to complete travelling through the amazing nation,
Here was I in Nashik boarding the train as Mumbai was my final destination.

I opened the window and felt the gentle movement of the train,
Gradually I took a walk down the memory lane.

"Just a few more hours and I'll be home."- I looked up in sky,
I felt the lakes, wind, rivers and snow clad mountains as the time would just fly.

But just then I could sense on me an ugly stare,
But to look into the eyes was something I couldn't dare.

In front were six eyeballs completely red sore,
The dirty appearance and the sick looks one couldn't ignore.

Their continuous act made me feel weird and I held my bag tightly,
Now my heart was pumping faster and I couldn't take it lightly.

It was December winter and I had enjoyed vacation thrills,
But then, while in the jungle and tunnels I could experience chills.

They looked on and on and on,
My pleaure by then had completely gone.

"Should I call the travelling companions? Or should I pull the chain?"
The night had may be planned a nightmare in the foreign country train.

I was shivering as cold breeze touched me, feeling fear and fright,
Don't know what I would have done if it went dark without any light.

'Excuse me Ma'am!', he said and occupied my next seat,
Tight fitting t-shirt and blue jeans appeared very neat.

I looked at a tall, fair and handsome man with almond eyes,
His hair shiny black, broad forehead with strong biceps, chest and thighs.

It was all very different and I could hardly react,
But as it is, I was undecisive about how to act?

Fifteen minutes later we had an eye contact and he gave me a curved smile,
His gentleness presented me comfort which was first in a little while.

He gave me his introduction as a Lecturer with his English sounding good,
I replied to him hesitantly and narrated the incident as softly as I could.

The stranger he was to me, but calmed me down,
Convincing me to feel safe without any grimness or frown.

He attracted friendly chats ignoring any friend or foe,
Carefully sharing laughs, he checked them head to toe.

We chatted…chatted… and the distance kept reducing every moment,
He would ask questions, I would answer followed by his comment.

By next 2 hours my feared eyes relaxed and were shut,
I guess journey's more than one hour got cut.

For I was tired, could manage an alert nap,
With my elbow on the window, palm supporting head and bag on lap.

Didn't notice when the train arrived and halted at the Thane junction,
The station noise woke me up, my body now being a normal function.

The remaining nervousness vanished as there were no stalking eyes and only visible was one's back,
The jerks were unboarding the train to never come back.

My stranger hero was missing and I guessed the loo,
But the train moved and maybe he had left too.

Ten minutes passed, he didn't return with the train in motion,
Regret, nervousness, annoyance- "Gosh!" My heart was filled with emotion.

An hour or so and at the Dadar station I got down,
How can I describe my journey? And with which adjective or noun?

Next journey to my home was flawless without any fear or fright,
Effortlessly I travelled to the airport and boarded my home flight.

Since home coming this Belgian girl recalls her fun, adventure and memories of vacation,
Only imagining how the 'hero' would have gazed at me with a sweet smile getting down at the station.

I wish I could have met him to wish final 'Good-Bye',
Could have thanked him looking eye to eye.

It was my sweet *'Maine Pyar Kiya'* moment for sure,
I felt like Simran of Raj, *'Dilwale Dulhaniya Le Jayenge'* was pure.

Why I say that today ? I thank the holy Nashik land for a new life,
The stranger happens to be my beloved husband and I'm the 'heroine' wife!

"What? How? When?" At the moment I won't tell,
Just know that 'heavens rang the wedding bell'.

Always had heard about 'soul-connections' and 'dreams come true',
I'm a firm believer today- *'Someone Somewhere Is Made For You'*.

Don't know if it was fortune, destiny, series of unique events or a real danger,
But surely know that it was the night when the God smiled at me, answered my prayers....**And I Met A Stranger!!**

Glossary- 1. 'Maine Pyar Kiya'- A Timeless Hindi Classic Movie of 1989

2. Dilwale Dulhania Le Jayenge (DDLJ)- A Hindi Romantic Blockbuster of 1995

3. Raj and Simran- The protagonist couple in DDLJ

The World Diaries

One day we woke up... (COVID 19)

Genre- Realism

Theme- Tragedy/Health

One day we woke up to find the world was not the same anymore,
We were locked in the houses as the invisible enemy waited outside the door.

It all was fine till 2019 as life was at it's peak,
But the unforeseen 2020 made future bleak.

The identity of the enemy was COVID-19- the virus,
The damage spread as forest fire without initial fuss.

The helpless governments opted for lockdowns,
First time in a century, citizens were caged in towns.

The busy streets of Rome were empty,
While a few days back, the movers were plenty.

Arc de Triomple (Paris) looked for visitors as there were hardly few,
The fashion capital (Milan) was deserted- a sight very new!

Berlin was lonely, Barcelona alone,
The silence was not silence, it was a moan.

The Pope's abode (Vatican City) was quiet,
The quietness appeared as the globe was under twilight.

The India Gate (Delhi) and Gateway of India (Mumbai) know only rush,
Even they wondered about the sudden hush.

The Madison Avenue (New York) loves displaying ads to the passers-by,
However, then the eyeballs were missing only boards remained under dark sky.

Before, Rio (Brazil) and Tel Aviv (Israel) had tourists, sea and beaches,
Cut to 2020, there were no tourists, remained only sea and beaches.

Whichever continent, whichever country, the stunning silence was inevitable,
The mild horror of an unseen threat outside was clearly visible.

As gloomy were times, the planet just prayed for emancipation,
Freedom from fear, hunger and death was the 'watery eyed' wish of every nation.

The Cross on the mountain (Arizona- USA)

Genre- Religion

Theme- Spirituality/Belief

Decades come and go in Arizona,
But the cross on the mountain stands tall.
Who erected it? Don't know!
Why? Don't know!
Only exist some stories, some assumptions.

It has seen time fly with winds,
On some days, it is under the dark cloudy sky,
On the others, it is under the clear blue sheet.
On some days, it enjoys the sun,
On the others, it is stubborn against furious gushing winds.

It is alone, it is isolated,
Seldom people visit this place.
It sees the red, brown and golden colours around it,
Doesn't complain about the coal-black nights.

People have different perceptions,
Some call it divine believing in Christ.
Some stay away sensing chills or untold fear.
Some are atheist, who don't bother to think.
And this is how 'God' too is looked upon!

For some he is divine to be loved,
For some he can't be reached,
While for some he doesn't exist!
It's a matter of perception! It is!!

A Rainy Day in Vietnam

Genre- Life

Theme- Rural Imagery/Monsoon

It's morning and it's still drizzling,
after a night of heavy showers.
The country side feels so serene,
as the traditional houses feel the music of droplets.
The sloping roofs spill down the water endlessly,
the roads appear shiny as washed.
I pass through the lanes which are quiet,
the lush green carpet spread all around.

Nearby flows the Hoai river stream which is ecstatic today,
with just a few boatmen rowing cautiously.
The white and grey clouds float like cotton,
embrace the mountains.

Sometimes appear the conical traditional caps,
and the children splashing water outside their homes.

In the market sits an old vendor,
His basket full of tropical fruits-
guavas, apples and the dragon fruits- all fresh.
He must sell for his bread and butter.
I stare at him for a while, wish for him and move ahead.
I am a tourist and my tour continues.....

England, World Cup and Uncle Sam

Genre- Story/Sports

Theme- Life/Emotions/Events

It was 1920 when Sam was born,
The World War was over and Depression was on,
In the school life Sam was a fabulous batter,
His first love was cricket not Rosey- it was indeed a serious matter!
He wished to see England rule the cricket world mate,
But he would have to wait!

It was 1975, ages later Sam was 'Uncle Sam' now,
Historic it was for England as the inaugural World Cup was there and how?
The family comprised wife Rosey, son and a daughter being complete,
At 55, he faced disappointment as West Indies won the trophy neat.
He wished to see England rule the cricket world mate,
But he would have to wait!

It was 1979, Uncle Sam almost retired,
England got it's first female Prime Minister, the criticism backfired.
Uncle Sam and Rosey enjoyed every laughter with grandkids both being innocent,
At 59, he was again heartbroken as West Indies was truly magnificient.
He wished to see England rule the cricket world mate,
But he would have to wait!

It was 1983, Uncle Sam needed stick to walk,
It had been celebrations in England as the Royal Wedding was the common talk.
Uncle Sam and aunt Rosey were going slow,
At 63, he cried again as it was Champ India's unmatched show.
He wished to see England rule the cricket world mate,
But he would have to wait!

It was 1987, Uncle Sam had weak eyes,
The soap opera 'East Enders' set new records with all going right.
Old aunt Rosey with dim eyes cared for her man more than before,
At 67, his dream was shattered again as 'Kangaroos' had their folk lore.
He wished to see England rule the cricket world mate,
But he would have to wait!
It was 2015, Uncle Sam could talk softly,

1991 to 2011- 6 World Cups were forgotten hardly.
Aunt Rosey had left for heavenly abode,
At 95, Uncle Sam was unmoved now as Australia played repeat mode.
He wished to see England rule the cricket world mate,
But he would have to wait!

It was 2019, Uncle Sam was now chairborne,
With T20 dominating, cricket was airborne.
Uncle Sam was loved by the children of his granddaughter and grandson,
At 99, finally his dream came true as England won!

His wrinkled lips laughed and eyes dropped tears,
His family surrounded and hugged him tight despite silly fears.
That night he tried to dance and even succeeded with some support,
May be it was his last opportunity said the medical report.

Next few days and months were cherry on top as Uncle Sam cut the cake,
The great batter once, scored a century on life's pitch without any break.

Six months later, one night Uncle Sam slept to remain forever cozy,

Years later were reunited in heavens Uncle Sam and Aunt Rosey!

Uncle Sam wished to see England rule the cricket world mate,

"His time had come and he didn't have to wait!.....

......His time had come and he didn't have to wait!!"

He almost robbed Messi (Argentina & France)

Genre- Sports

Theme- Player/Emotions/Legacy

Event- Football World Cup Final 2022

The world watched the final test,
Who among the two would be the 'best of the best'?

Millions prayed for Argentina's victory as it was 'his' last chance,
Yet defending champ stood tall; it was called France.

Globally speaking, the support ratio was ninety:ten,
Argentina was the fan favourite whether women or men.

11 warriors on the field on one side,
11 gladiators on the field on the other- one last ride!

Match started and audience roared,
Clock ticked and sweat poured.

King Messi scored a couple of goals giving loud shout,
Argentinian win looked certain, less was doubt.

Yet destiny had some other plans; Messi needed to wait more,
In stepped 'French Prince' Mbappe to play hardcore.

The South American giant was denied it's day,
Whenever they touched the trophy, the French warrior came in the way.

With King Messi's two goals fans couldn't ask for more,
But the lone warrior Mbappe added a royal hat-trick to the score.

The nail bites must have set records around the globe,
Eagerly watching were Brazil, Germany or the country of the Pope.

What looked like a cakewalk was a thorny path,
"La Albiceleste" might not have enjoyed the champagne bath.

It was not Argentina vs France anymore dear,
Renaming Argentina vs Mbappe makes it crystal clear.

The extra time ended; both finalists with 3 goals each,
The cup was now slipping away which was within the reach.

The dust settled only after the penalty shootout,
Argentina won; the World Cup ended clearing every doubt.

Every player on the field had tears of their own; no need to borrow,
The difference being, some had tears of happiness while some had those of sorrow.

King Messi concluded his illustrious journey with mixed emotions,
Within seconds, he celebrated every moment on the field involving all motions.

But in the middle of the field the heartbroken French prince lied down,
It was not his day, the destiny denied him the royal crown and gown.

Buenos Aires rejoiced, Paris cried,
But 22 mothers and fathers felt the highest pride.

The world said goodbye to the king and welcomed the prince,
It was the night that the king met the prince.

Millions of prayers answered and retired legend Messi,

But Mbappe's legacy commenced as <u>he almost robbed Messi!</u>

<u>*Glossary*</u>- *La Albiceleste'*- Name of Argentinian football team

Straight from the Heart

'Parvati is Shiva and Shiva is Parvati'

I waited for you as dry desert for rain,
On lonely nights, I gazed at the moon with endless pain.

It was not a separation of few years but of ages,
It's not decades, those were lifetime's pages.

But I never broke my promise which I made births ago,
I stayed chaste without letting purity go.

You too followed the same,
I found your virgin body and virgin soul as you came.

It's not human, it's divine,
I'm yours and you are mine.

The days and nights all celebrate our union on earth,
The stars, moon and sun witness our holy wedding-our rebirth.

Yes, history repeats itself,

Parvati waited for Shiva as Shiva waited for Parvati,

And when they met,

Parvati is Shiva and Shiva is Parvati!